To sleepy folks who read to sleepy darlings
—E.H.F.

For summer evenings on the porch, crickets, stargazing,
and all the small things that are so very important
—C.D.

Text copyright © 2014 by Edith Hope Fine
Jacket art and interior illustrations copyright © 2014 by Christopher Denise

Visit us on the Web! randomhouse.com/kids

Educators and librarians, for a variety of teaching tools, visit us at RHTeachersLibrarians.com

Library of Congress Cataloging-in-Publication Data
Fine, Edith Hope.
Sleepytime me / by Edith Hope Fine ; illustrated by Christopher Denise. — First edition.
pages cm.
Summary: "From the great expanse of the darkening sky filled with stars, to the softening sounds of city and farm quieting down for the night,
the perspective comes closer to reveal the end of day at home and then the child snuggling into bed." — Provided by publisher.
ISBN 978-0-449-81062-0 (trade) — ISBN 978-0-375-97147-1 (lib. bdg.) — ISBN 978-0-375-98135-7 (ebook)
[1. Stories in rhyme. 2. Bedtime—Fiction.] I. Denise, Christopher, illustrator. II. Title. PZ8.3.F59Sl 2014   [E]—dc23   2012041934

MANUFACTURED IN MALAYSIA
10 9 8 7 6 5 4 3 2 1
First Edition

Sleepytime Me

by Edith Hope Fine

illustrated by Christopher Denise

RANDOM HOUSE NEW YORK

Splashy sunset
paints the sky.
Shy moon tiptoes,
climbs up high.

Daylight's fading.
Stars grow bright.
Darkness glowing.
Velvet night.

Yawn around, yawn around, sleepytime sky.

Chickens settle.
Kittens purr.
Piglets whuffle.
Puppies stir.

Downy ducklings,
find your nest.
Burrow, bunnies,
time for rest.

Yawn around, yawn around, sleepytime farm.

Nighttime gathers.
Work is done.
Headlights shimmer.
Streetlights on.

Freight trains whisper.
Buses roam.
Big trucks rumble.
Cars head home.

Yawn around, yawn around, sleepytime town.

Wash the dishes.
Sweep the floor.
Toys to toy box.
Close the door.

Windows shuttered.
Curtains drawn.
Bath time. Book time.
Night-lights on.

Yawn around, yawn around, sleepytime house.

Yawning, yawning.
Snuggle close.
Hugs and kisses.
Start to doze.

Teddy. Blankie.
Jammies. Bed.
Snuggly pillow.
Sleepyhead.

Yawn around, yawn around, sleepytime me.

Night-night. Sleep tight. Sleep tight.